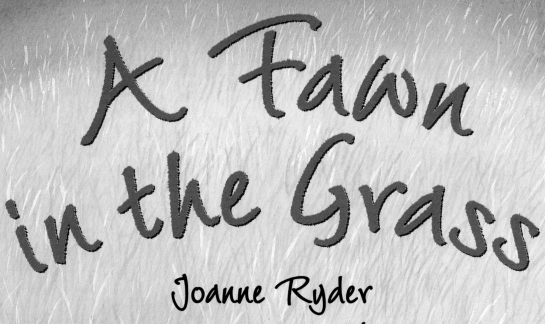

A Fawn in the Grass

Joanne Ryder

ILLUSTRATED BY Keiko Narahashi

HENRY HOLT AND COMPANY · NEW YORK

Henry Holt and Company, LLC
Publishers since 1866
115 West 18th Street, New York, New York 10011

Henry Holt is a registered trademark of Henry Holt and Company, LLC
Text copyright © 2001 by Joanne Ryder
Illustrations copyright © 2001 by Keiko Narahashi
All rights reserved.
Published in Canada by Fitzhenry & Whiteside Ltd.,
195 Allstate Parkway, Markham, Ontario L3R 4T8.

Library of Congress Cataloging-in-Publication Data
Ryder, Joanne. A fawn in the grass / Joanne Ryder; illustrated by Keiko Narahashi.
Summary: Rhyming text lists a series of animals in their natural habitats,
from a fawn in the grass and a snail underneath a leaf to a buzzing bee and
two racing hummingbirds. [1. Animals—Fiction. 2. Stories in rhyme.]
I. Narahashi, Keiko, ill. II. Title. PZ8.3.R9595 Faw 2001 [E]—dc21 00-24284
ISBN 0-8050-6236-X / First Edition—2001 / Designed by Donna Mark
Printed in the United States of America on acid-free paper. ∞

1 3 5 7 9 10 8 6 4 2

The artist used gouache and watercolor on Arches watercolor paper
to create the illustrations for this book.

To Cory, Lee, and Matthew

—J. R.

To Peter

—K. N.

There's a fawn in the grass,
watching me as I pass.

I am silent and slow
as it watches me go.

There's a trail on a leaf

and a snail underneath.

There are treasures to see
hiding all around me.

There's a nose in a hole—

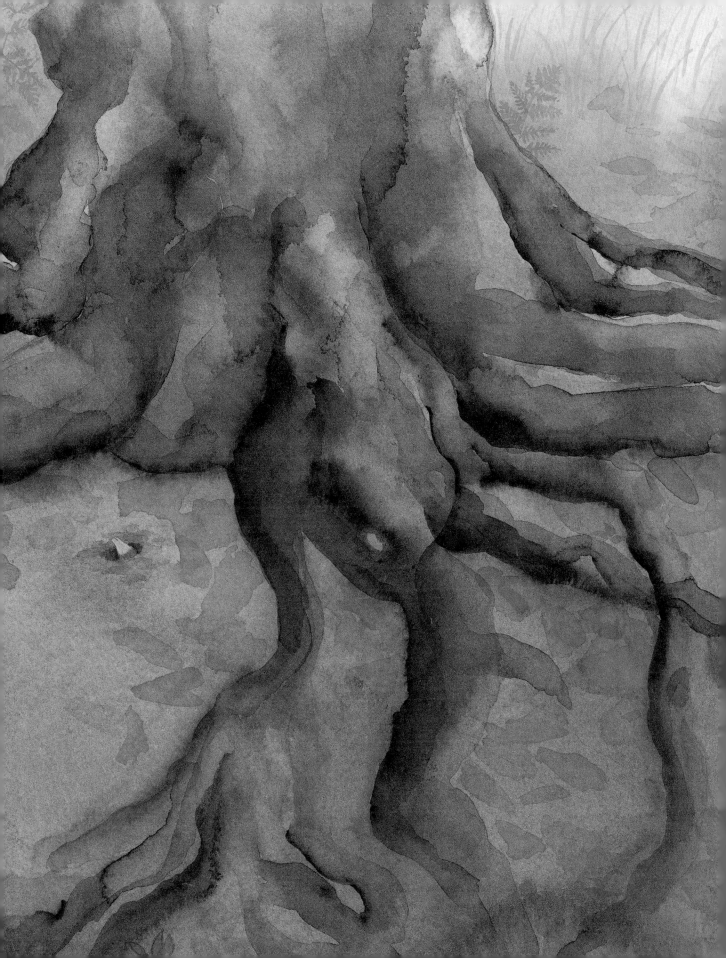

and the nose is a mole!

There's a speck in the sky

as a hawk circles high.

There's a lizard who creeps
past another who sleeps.

I see more things each day
as new friends come my way.

There's a worm on a string,
who is swaying in space.

There's a white butterfly

on a circle of lace.

There's a squirrel who clings
to the side of a tree.

There's a flash of a jay,

and the buzz of a bee.

There's a blur and a whir

as two hummingbirds race.

There's a smile on my face
as I peek, as I pass. . . .

There's a fawn in the grass.

The Fawn in Our Grass

One spring night a doe leaped over our fence and gave birth to a fawn in our yard. The doe left each morning, but the fawn would stay, hidden in the grass. Unless it moved or squeaked, it was hard to find. And we let the grass grow tall so it could hide safely. The fawn stayed in our yard for several weeks until one day it left with its mother.

I loved walking outside and seeing the tiny fawn, and I wrote this book while it was living nearby. Can you find the fawn in the picture below?